"SMELLY" KELLY AND HIS SUPER SENSES

How James Kelly's Nose Saved the New York City Subway

Beth Anderson

Illustrated by
Jenn Harney

CALKINS CREEK
An Imprint of Boyds Mills & Kane
New York

James Kelly smelled everything.

Rats in the shed.

Circus elephants a mile away.

Tomorrow's rain.

But what good was an extraordinary nose? He'd rather have amazing strength or astonishing speed. Something that would make him special.

He gazed over the rolling hills. His future was out there. He could almost smell it.

James arrived in New York City with nothing but a suitcase and a keen sense of smell.

The metropolis hummed. Buildings stretched to the sky. Scents familiar and foreign wafted in the breeze.

James set out to find a job, but, as always, his incredible nose proved troublesome.

Fish market—*no!*

Sanitation—*no!*

Meat packing—*no!*

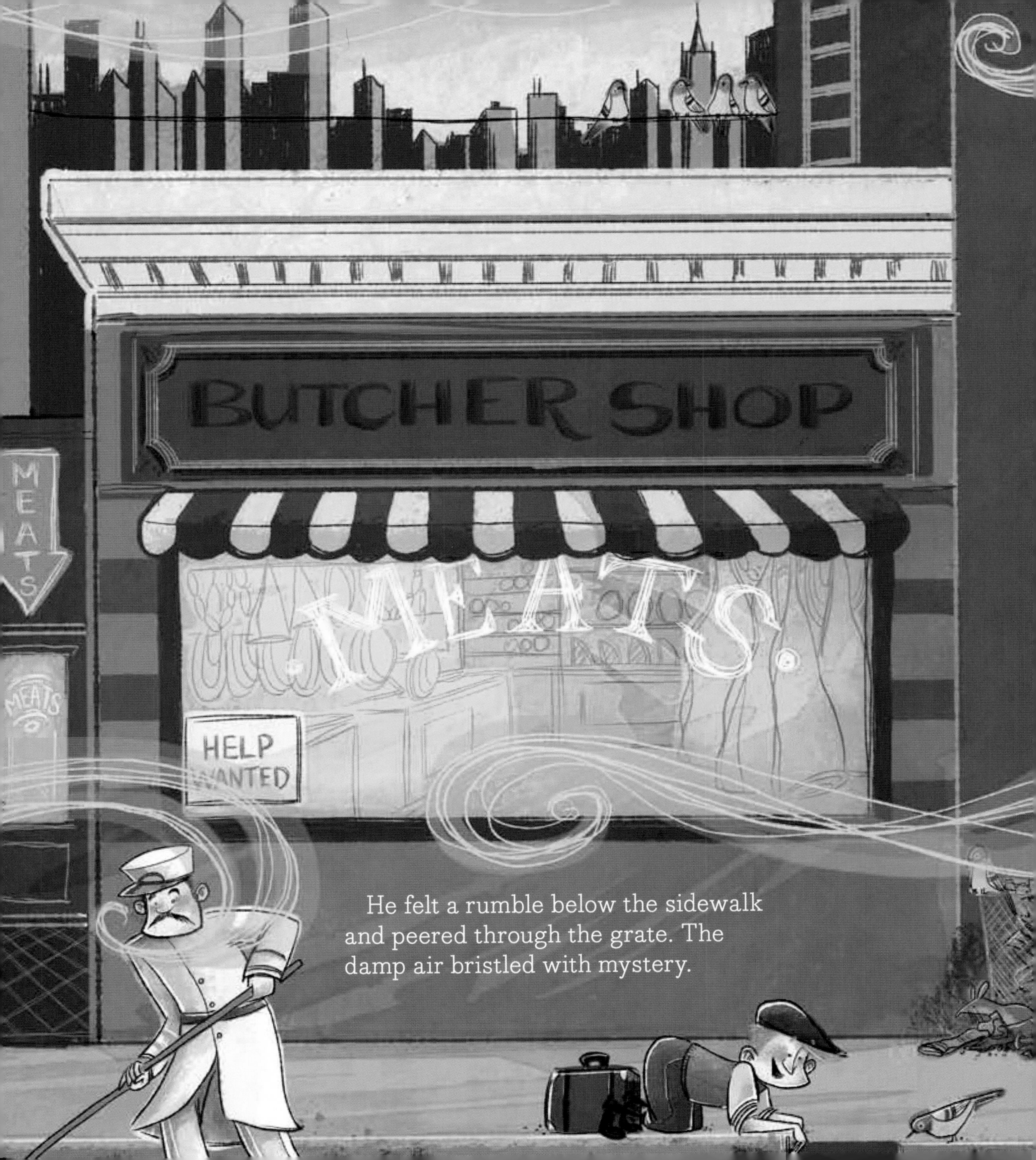

He felt a rumble below the sidewalk and peered through the grate. The damp air bristled with mystery.

The subway—*yes!*

Mild-mannered James Kelly descended into an underground world layered with cables and wires, gas pipes and steam lines, water mains and sewers. Where trains rushed past, powered by the sizzling electricity of the third rail. Where a nick, a crack, a break, a spark could wreak havoc.

Kelly's nose twitched as the
maintenance crew tightened bolts on the track.
He followed *whifffffs* no one else smelled . . .

. . . discovered leaks lurking out of sight . . .

Word spread. James Kelly had a knack for leaks.
And soon, a new name: *Smelly Kelly*.

With such an honor came great responsibility.

He read and researched, anxious to show he was more than just a super-sniffer. He learned about a chemical powder that colored water yellow and meters that measured invisible gases

Meanwhile . . . behind a wall in the Hotel New Yorker . . .

Maids pinched their noses. Guests fled. Engineers analyzed and pondered, but they couldn't figure out where the leak was coming from.

And just like with every other obnoxious stink, mysterious leak, and suspicious noise in the city, everyone blamed the subway.

The hotel manager phoned the transit office.
Eager to see if rumors about Kelly were true, the subway's chief engineer summoned the infamous nose to the scene.

Smelly Kelly sniffed the water stain, searching for the most odiferous spot. But he couldn't pinpoint the break in the pipe.

Faced with failure, he pulled a bag of yellow powder from his pocket, poured it into the toilet, and . . .

. . . flushed . . . flushed . . . flushed.

His studying paid off! Kelly pointed to a yellow spot growing on the wall. *There* was the break.

After that, Smelly Kelly "was in leaks for keeps," the subway's first official leak detective. He vowed no dangers would go undetected on his watch.

Maybe, his incredible nose *could* make him special.

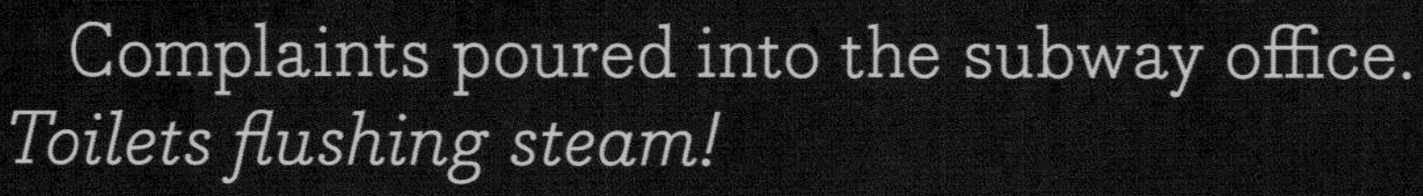

Complaints poured into the subway office. *Toilets flushing steam!*

Smelly Kelly rushed to the 42nd Street men's room.

He followed the pipes . . . up and down ladders . . . through passageways.

SHOOOOOSH!

A broken steam line blasted water pipes.

Kelly shook his head. Someone could've been burned. Sniffing wasn't enough. He needed to listen, to hear sounds no one else heard.

Smelly Kelly trained his ears to pick up a telltale hiss . . . a rhythmic drip.

But he needed something stronger—to magnify and transmit sounds . . . like a telephone or stethoscope.

Kelly headed to the shop and experimented into the wee hours of the night.

His tool bag bulging with new gadgets, Kelly walked ten miles of track each day. He astounded onlookers as he rushed from one station to another—defending the reputation of the subway, tackling toxic spills, and capturing clogs.

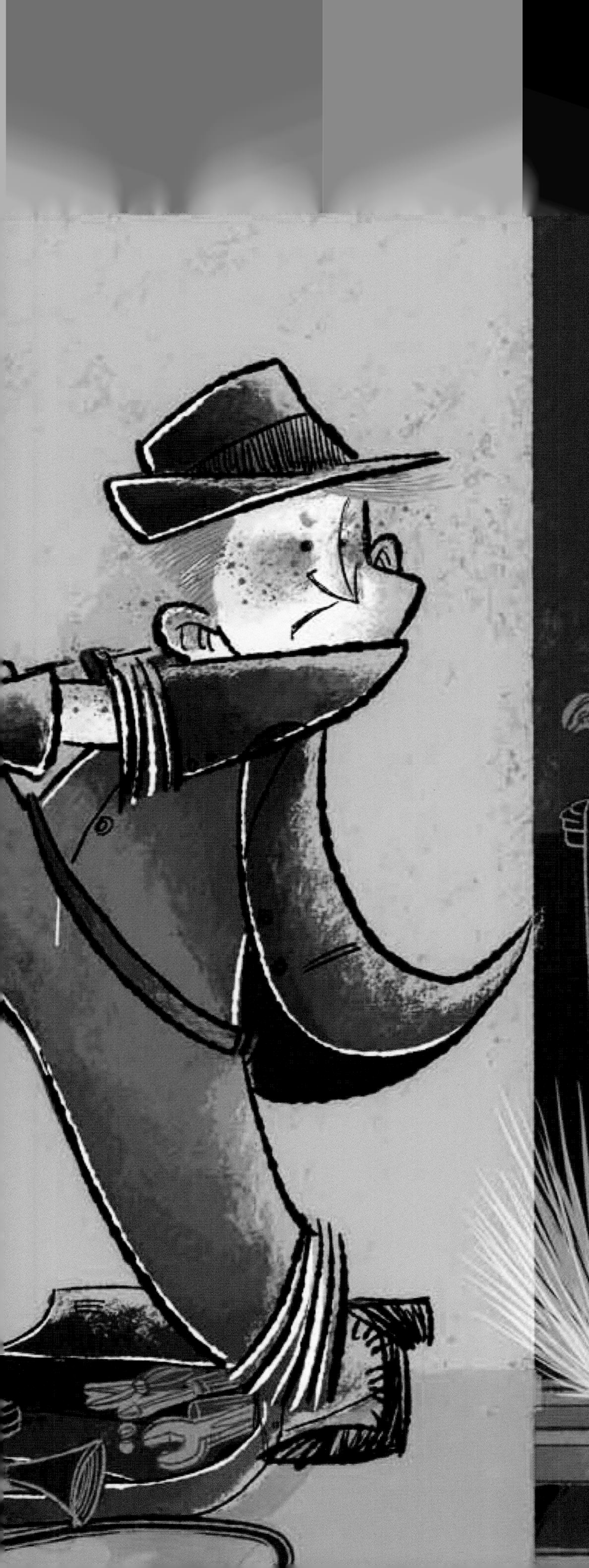

But his super-senses were powerless against the electricity of the third rail.

As the city grew, so did the subway and the underground legend of Smelly Kelly. But keeping 247 miles of track safe by himself was impossible.

Exhausted, he paused and peered through the crowd gathered at a movie poster. Even superheroes needed help.

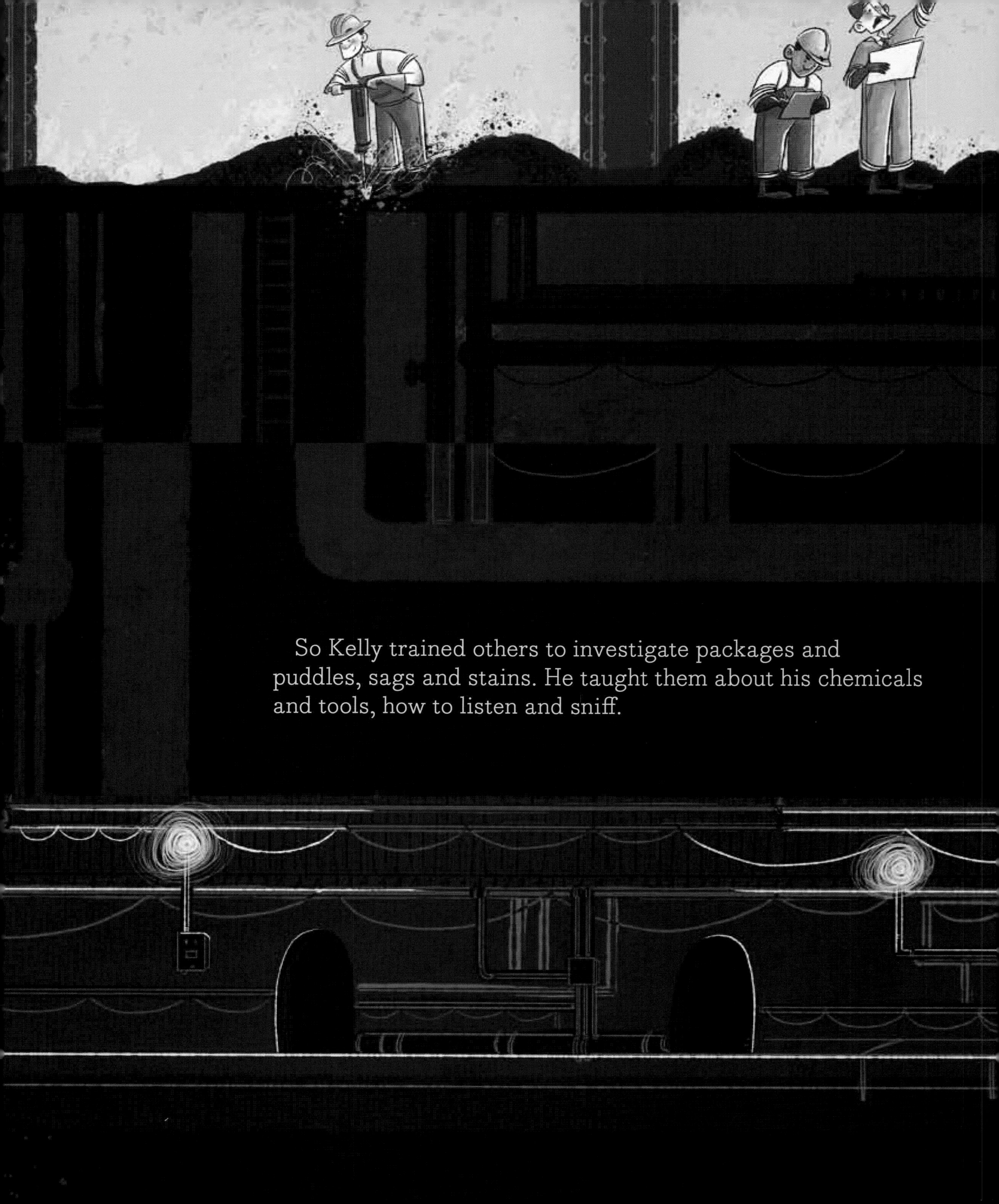

So Kelly trained others to investigate packages and puddles, sags and stains. He taught them about his chemicals and tools, how to listen and sniff.

All the while, jackhammers and steam shovels dug into the earth, burying storage tanks, anchoring skyscrapers, weaving more wires and pipes into the maze beneath the streets.

RRRRRRRING!

Kelly leaped out of bed to answer the phone.

Emergency!

Tar-like smell!

Ready in ten seconds flat, he grabbed his tool bag and raced to Midtown.

He identified the culprit in a single sniff: "Gasoline."

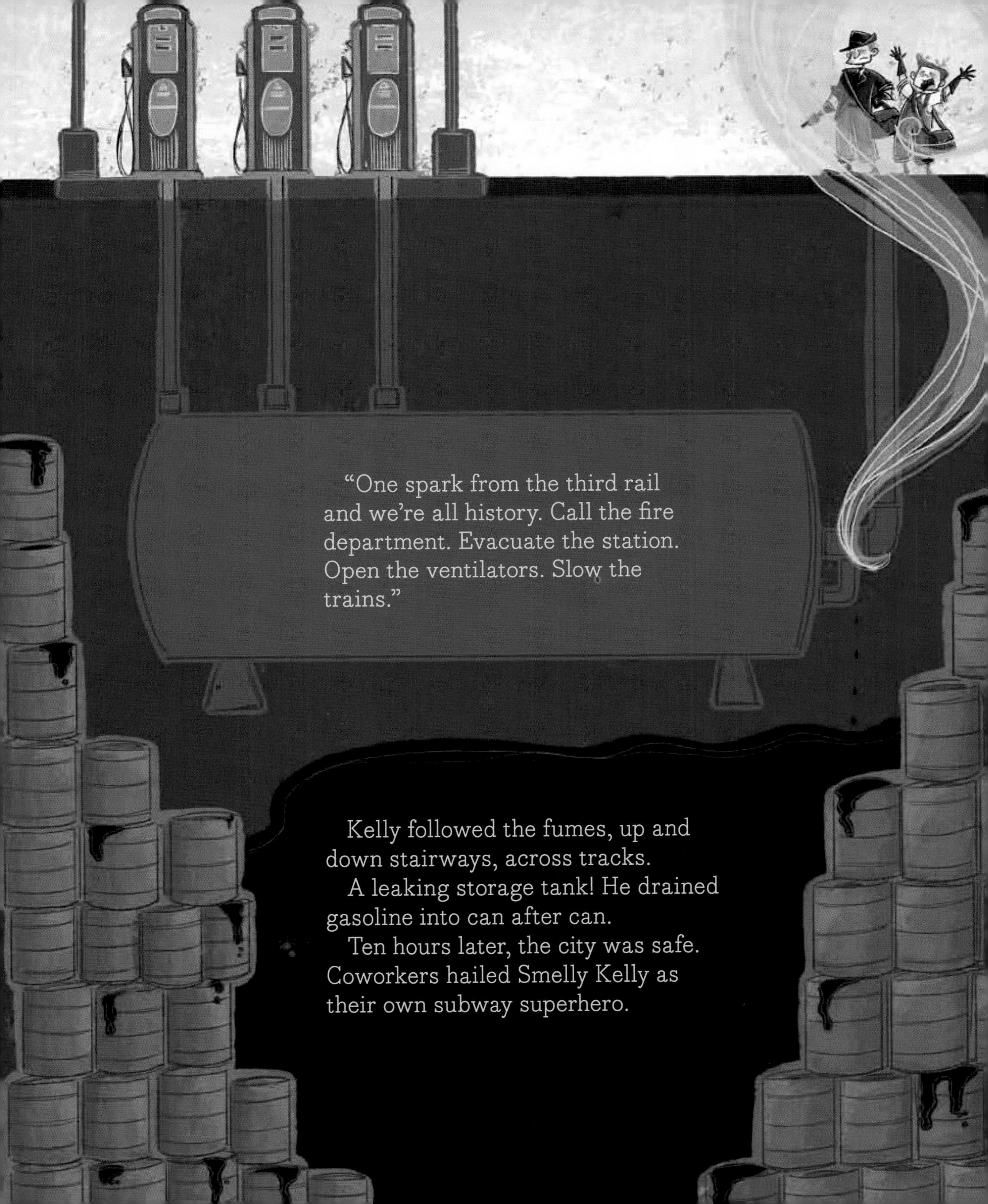

"One spark from the third rail and we're all history. Call the fire department. Evacuate the station. Open the ventilators. Slow the trains."

Kelly followed the fumes, up and down stairways, across tracks.

A leaking storage tank! He drained gasoline into can after can.

Ten hours later, the city was safe. Coworkers hailed Smelly Kelly as their own subway superhero.

But when the most colossal, most nauseating, most nose-scrunching stench ever to hit the subway filled the 42nd Street station, everyone thought Kelly's sniffer had met its match.

A train arrived, and Kelly stepped out.

WHOOOOOOF!

The odor nearly blew him back into the car. Kelly frowned. It was familiar . . . something from his childhood. He lifted his nose . . . circled the platform. "Elephants." He was certain.

He climbed up to the street and surveyed the surroundings.

His eyes settled on the new Hippodrome Center. He nodded, remembering the grand old building that once stood there—where elephants performed. Workers had torn it down, but they must have left something behind.

Kelly held his aquaphone against a fire hydrant.

Then, with his stethoscope, he followed the hiss, down and up manholes, along sidewalks.
Aha! A broken water main.

SSSSSSSS . . .

. . .soaking long-buried elephant manure.

Once again, Smelly Kelly saved the day!
Still, most people didn't know about the fumes that never exploded. Or the dripping water that never caused cave-ins. Or the super-sniffer whose workday never ended.

Heading home, Kelly stood at the front of the subway car. His nose twitched, his ears strained, his eyes searched.

Suddenly, ahead, a man fell from the platform onto the tracks.

The motorman braked . . . wheels screeched.

Kelly jumped down and peered beneath the car. The man, unconscious, lay between the rails. Inches from the underside of the car. Inches from the electrified third rail.

Kelly's extraordinary nose and ears were worthless.

But he sensed something deep inside. He'd felt it before.

Smelly Kelly listened to his heart. He followed it through doubts, past fear.

He took off his coat, crawled under the car, and pinned the man down. If either moved, they'd both be in danger.

Slowly, the motorman backed the train over the men.

Kelly pressed down as the car passed over him, so close he barely breathed.

Moments later, they were clear, and Kelly helped the man up.

The crowd gasped. Then cheered.

Smelly Kelly smiled at everyone.

The motorman.

The man he'd rescued.

The people on the platform.

Finally, he understood. He *did* have more than an incredible nose! Something better than amazing strength or astonishing speed. It was the force that pushed him . . . to study, invent, and risk his life. His special power was *inside*.

James Kelly gazed at the waiting passengers. He would bet each person had something special inside. He could almost smell it.

So you've got to figure the leak before it figures you and blows everything to kingdom come.

—Smelly Kelly

Author's Note

James Patrick Kelly was born in Ireland in 1898. At age sixteen, he worked with his uncle, a well-digger, finding water with a divining rod. This may have been an early clue that his senses were keener than most. When he was eighteen, he joined the British Navy and served as a hydrophone operator, locating enemy submarines in World War I. After the war, he emigrated to the United States and settled in New York City.

Smelly Kelly, also known as "Leaky," "Sniffy," and "The Sniffer," was good-natured and hardworking. Each day on the job, Kelly discovered an average of eight leaks as he walked ten miles of track. It's estimated that in his career he covered nearly 100,000 miles on foot and trained sixty assistants. "Sniffing" was more than a job to Kelly. To him, it was an art, essential to keeping the city safe. Throughout his career, Kelly remained on emergency call 24/7. The chairman of the Transit Authority once said, "In thirty years in the railroad business, I have never before encountered a man with the peculiar talents of Mr. Kelly."

In addition to his perfect record saving the subway from dangers, James Kelly received two commendations for heroism. In 1939, he grabbed hold of a worker and prevented him from falling forward into an onrushing train. The final incident in the story, saving the man from under the train, occurred in 1943.

Near the end of Kelly's career, the gas company began using dogs to detect underground fumes. When someone asked him if he was afraid he'd be replaced by a dog, he laughed and responded, "Dogs are not allowed in the subway."

Kelly's Tools

The yellow powder that Kelly used in 1932 at the Hotel New Yorker was uranine, a chemical used to stain water yellow. He is said to be the first to use uranine to detect leaks. Seven years later, in WWII, it was used to help search-planes locate pilots who had been shot down over the ocean.

The aquaphone, one of Kelly's inventions, was a telephone receiver with a hollow rod soldered to the disk that picks up sound. Records indicate that early versions had a copper wire instead of the rod. He generally used this tool to listen to fire hydrants. A hissing sound indicated a nearby leak in the line.

When he needed a tool more sensitive to sound than the aquaphone, Kelly used his own version of a stethoscope. He soldered a pointed, eight-inch steel rod onto the stethoscope's disk and used it to listen along sidewalks and pipes.

As shown in the gasoline scene, Kelly used an explosimeter, an instrument that measures the amount of gases in the air that might explode. Explosimeters had been in use for more than a century.

Today, though various forms of technology are used to detect and measure leaks and fumes in the subway, workers still depend on sharp ears and a keen sense of smell.

The Underground World

Besides the subway, enough wire, cable, and pipes snake through the underground of New York City to wrap around the earth more than 2,334 times!

The *New York Times* reported:

- 6,400 miles of natural-gas mains
- 7,500 miles of sewer lines, some more than one hundred years old
- 58 million feet of conduit carrying telecommunication lines for TV, telephones, and internet
- More than one hundred miles of steam lines
- Almost 89,000 miles of electrical cables
- 6,800 miles of water pipes, some more than one hundred years old

A Note About the Research

Beyond the information he shared in four interviews, little is known about James Kelly. And it was two years into the publishing process that the fourth article surfaced. The transit employee newsletter mentions his family, confirming that census data I had found was really him. Suddenly, James Kelly was even more real. He had a wife named Anna; three sons, James, Thomas, and Alfred; and a daughter Margaret, nicknamed Peggy, who didn't appreciate having a father everyone called "Smelly." Census records for 1930 and 1940 list his birthplace, addresses in New York City, that he had a 7th grade education, and earnings of $1,820 in 1939. Ordinary details of an extraordinary man.

Since I had no information on his childhood, I imagined a boy growing up in Ireland with a super-sensitive nose. A boy who might have wished for a more "heroic" physical talent. And a nose that could be more of a problem than a blessing. Though the beginning employs a bit of fiction, the subway incidents in the story are true. The scene about the leak in the gasoline storage tank combines details from two of Kelly's experiences.

Like most superheroes, James Patrick Kelly remains a bit of a mystery. The information we have is enough that we can marvel at his super-senses, admire his ingenuity, laugh at his strange experiences, and applaud his courage. We can also wonder how many more heroes are out there, disguised as ordinary people.

Bibliography

All quotations used in the book can be found in the following source marked with an asterisk (*).

Primary Sources

*Daley, Robert. *The World Beneath the City*. Philadelphia: Lippincott, 1959.

Esterow, Milton. "Subway Sniffer Leads Mole's Life, Hunting Aromas on 247-Mile Beat; PROTECTING THE SUBWAY RIDERS HERE." *New York Times*, 25 July 1950: 29.

"Leaky Kelly." *New Yorker*, 26 July 1941: 8–9.

"Man With a Nose." *Transit*, February 1955: 12–13.

Secondary Sources

Heller, Vivian. *The City Beneath Us: Building the New York Subways*. New York: W.W. Norton, 2004.

"Industrial Map of New York City: Showing Manufacturing Industries, Concentration, Distribution, Character / Prepared by the Industrial Bureau of the Merchants' Association of New York." NYPL Map Warper: Map 14895. New York Public Library.

Interborough Rapid Transit. *The New York Subway: Its Construction and Equipment*. New York: Fordham University Press, 1991.

Misra, Tanvi. "This 19th Century 'Stench Map' Shows How Smells Reshaped New York City." CityLab. The Atlantic Monthly Group, 27 Mar. 2015. citylab.com/equity/2015/03/this-19th-century-stench-map-shows-how-smells-reshaped-new-york-city/388727/.

Rueb, Emily S. "Why Are the Streets Always Under Construction?" *New York Times*. 18 Aug. 2016. nytimes.com/interactive/2016/08/18/nyregion/new-york-101-streets-repair-and-maintenance.html.

Thompson, Emily, and Scott Mahoy. "The Roaring Twenties: An Interactive Exploration of the Historical Soundscape of New York City." *Vect*[illegible] vectorsdev.usc.edu/NYCsound/777b.html

Further Resources

Books

Corey, Shana, and Red Nose Studio. *The Secret Subway*. New York: Schwartz & Wade. 2016.
Guillain, Charlotte, and Yuval Zommer. *The Street Beneath My Feet*. London: words and pictures. 2017.
Ponzi, Emiliano. *The Great New York Subway Map*. New York: Museum of Modern Art. 2018.

Websites*

Building the first New York City subway (also click on "Learn More"): pbs.org/video/american-experience-constructing-new-yorks-first-subway/
New York City Transit Museum: nytransitmuseum.org

Acknowledgments

Many thanks to Joseph Cunningham, engineering and rail historian, and Rebecca Haggerty, Research Archivist at the New York Transit Museum, for answering my questions and helping me understand and envision James Kelly's work in the subway. Thanks also to my many critique partners who use their super-writer senses to provide valuable feedback and continual support.

**Websites active at time of publication*

With gratitude to all the courageous, hardworking immigrants who have crossed seas and borders in search of a better life, given the very best of themselves, and made their new country a better place for all —*BA*

For Kevin—*JH*

Picture Credits

Courtesy of New York Transit Museum: 36

Calkins Creek
An imprint of Boyds Mills & Kane, a division of Astra Publishing House
calkinscreekbooks.com
Printed in China

ISBN: 978-1-68437-399-4
Library of Congress Control Number: 2019953789

First edition
10 9 8 7 6 5 4 3 2 1

The text is set in Bodoni Egyptian Pro.
The illustrations are digital.

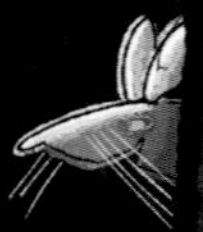